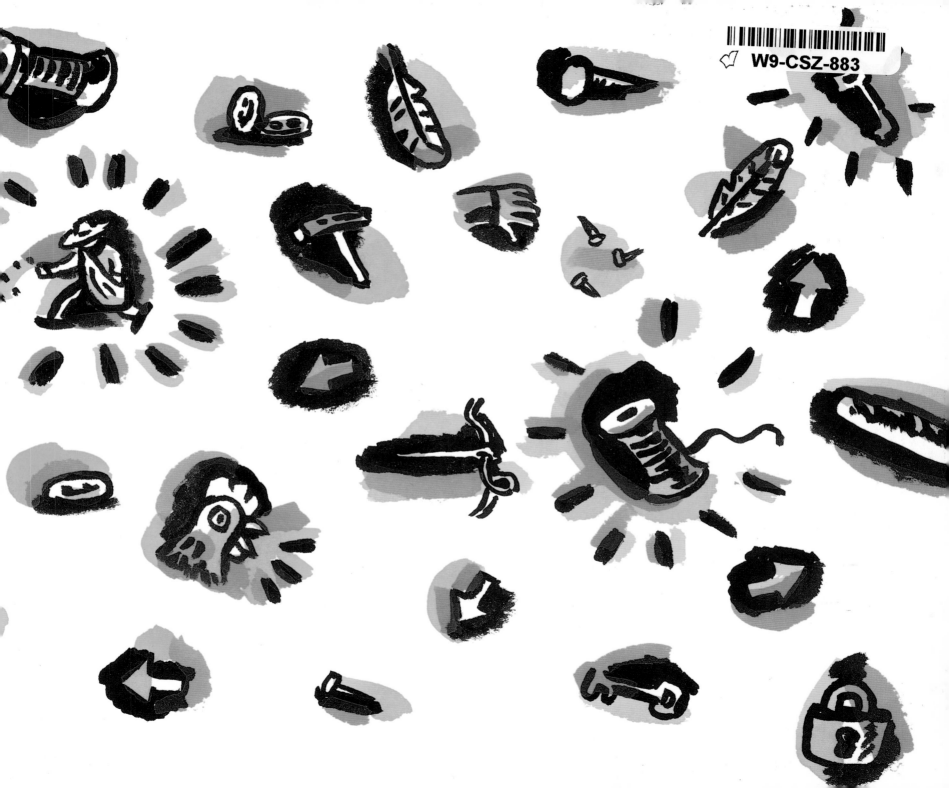

# PETER and the TALKING SHOES

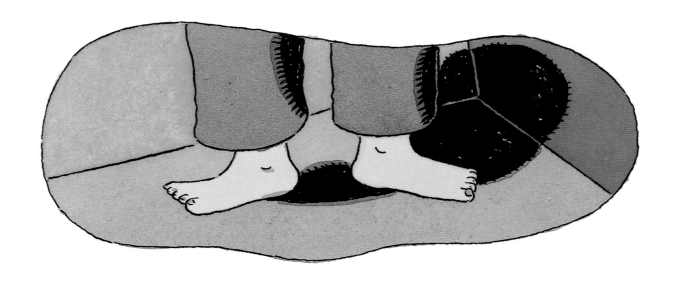

**By Kate Banks • illustrated by Marc Rosenthal**

Alfred A. Knopf • New York

THIS IS A BORZOI BOOK PUBLISHED BY ALFRED A. KNOPF, INC.

Text copyright © 1994 by Katherine Anne Banks. Illustrations copyright © 1994 by Marc Rosenthal.
All rights reserved under International and Pan-American Copyright Conventions. Published
in the United States of America by Alfred A. Knopf, Inc., New York, and simultaneously in Canada by Random
House of Canada Limited, Toronto. Distributed by Random House, Inc., New York.

Library of Congress Cataloging-in-Publication Data: Banks, Kate.   Peter and the Talking Shoes.
Katherine Anne Banks ; illustrated by Marc Rosenthal.   p.   cm.   Summary: Peter, the son of a music
man, is led on an adventure by the voice of his talking shoes.
ISBN 0-394-82723-6 (trade)   —   ISBN 0-394-92723-0 (lib. bdg.)
[1. Shoes—Fiction]  I. Rosenthal, Marc, 1949-  , ill.  II. Title.  PZ7.B22594Pe  1993  [E]—dc20  90-45278
Manufactured in the United States of America   10 9 8 7 6 5 4 3 2 1
Designed by Eileen Rosenthal

For Peter Anton
K.B.

For Frances
M.R.

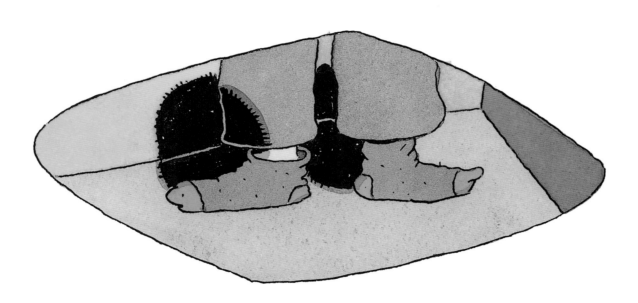

**P**eter had a new pair of shoes.
They weren't really new. They were brown,
and worn, and rough at the edges.
"But they are good and sturdy," said Peter's
father as he handed them to him.

Peter put them on. He tied the laces and wiggled his toes.
"They sure feel good," he said.
"Then you'd better try them out," said Peter's father.
He handed Peter three coins.
"Run down to the baker and buy us
a loaf of bread," he said.

So off Peter ran in his new pair of shoes.

"Good morning," said the baker.
"I'd like a loaf of bread," said Peter. He reached into his pocket.
  It was empty. "Oh!" he said. "I've lost my coins."
"Well," said the baker, "I've lost my feather. And I can't bake bread as
  light as a feather without one. If you find me a feather, then
  I'll give you a loaf of bread."
"All right," said Peter, and he left the baker.
"But where will I find a feather?" he wondered.

"I'll tell you where to find a feather," said a rough voice from below.
  Peter looked down. He looked at his shoes.
"Did you say something?" he asked.
"Feathers grow on the cock that crows in the field of one who sows seeds,"
  said the shoes.

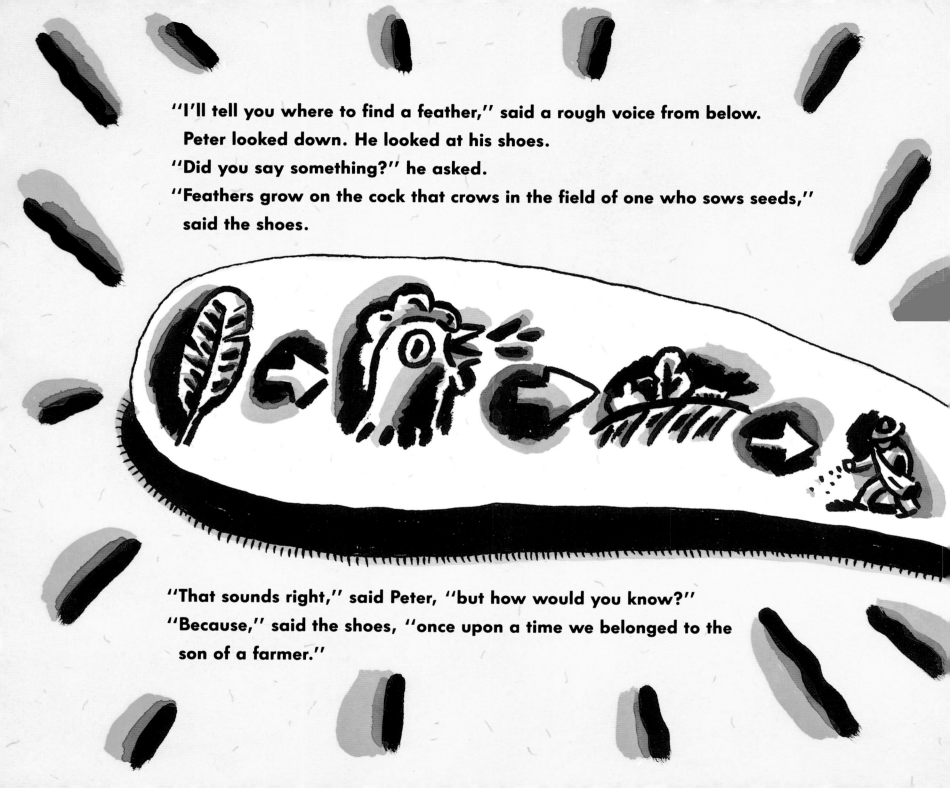

"That sounds right," said Peter, "but how would you know?"
"Because," said the shoes, "once upon a time we belonged to the
  son of a farmer."

So off Peter went to see the farmer.

"I need a feather," said Peter.

"Well, you can't have a feather for nothing," said the farmer.

"Look here, I need some buttons to hold up my pants. If you can get me some buttons, then I'll give you a feather."

"All right," said Peter, and he left the farmer.

"But where will I find some buttons?" he asked.

"Running from the needle, racing
round the thread of one
who mends trousers," said the shoes.
Peter looked down at his feet.
"You were right before,"
he said, "but why should I
believe you now?"
"Because," said the shoes, "we once
belonged to the son of a tailor."
So off Peter went to see the tailor.

"What can I do for you?" asked the tailor.
"I need some buttons," said Peter.
"And I need a nail to fix my roof," said the
tailor. "I'll tell you what. If you find me a
nail, then I'll give you some buttons."
"All right," said Peter, and he
left the tailor.

"But where will I find a nail?" he asked,
and he looked down at his feet.
"Hiding in the pocket furthest from the hand
of one who holds the hammer," said the shoes.

"That sounds right," said Peter.
"But are you sure?"
"We should know," said the shoes. "Once we
belonged to the son of a carpenter."
So off Peter went to see the carpenter.
"That's a fine house," said Peter.
"Yes," said the carpenter, "but I need a key
to get in the door."

"If I find you a key," said Peter, "will you give me a nail?"

"All right," said the carpenter, and Peter left her.

"But where will I find a key?" he asked the shoes.

"Dancing on a ring wrapped around the wrist of one
   who turns locks," said the shoes.

"That sounds right," said Peter.

"But how do you know?"

"Because," said the shoes,

"we once belonged to the son
   of a locksmith."

So off Peter went to see the locksmith.

"What a lot of keys!" said Peter. "Could you give me just one?"

"I'll gladly give you one," said the locksmith, "if you can show me how to make them jingle a tune."

Peter looked down at his shoes. "How can I make keys jingle a tune?" he asked. But the shoes said nothing.

"Hmmm," Peter thought to himself. Then suddenly he cried, "I can make keys jingle, for I am the son of a musician!" Peter set to work while the shoes watched. And in no time at all the keys were jingling a tune.

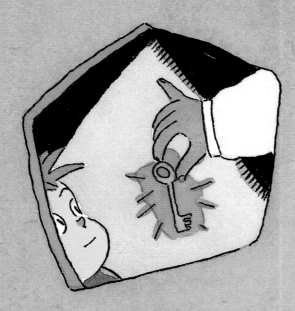

"Well done,"
said the locksmith, and he
handed Peter a key.

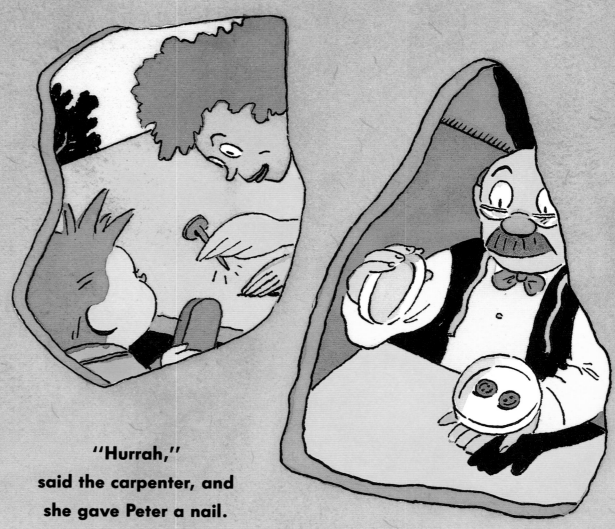

"Hurrah,"
said the carpenter, and
she gave Peter a nail.

"Thank you," said the tailor,
and he found some buttons.

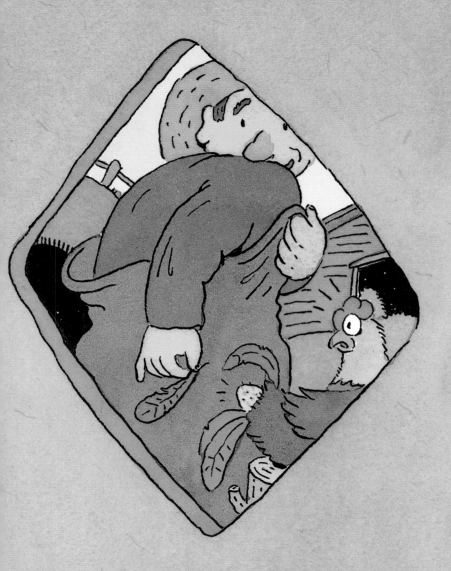

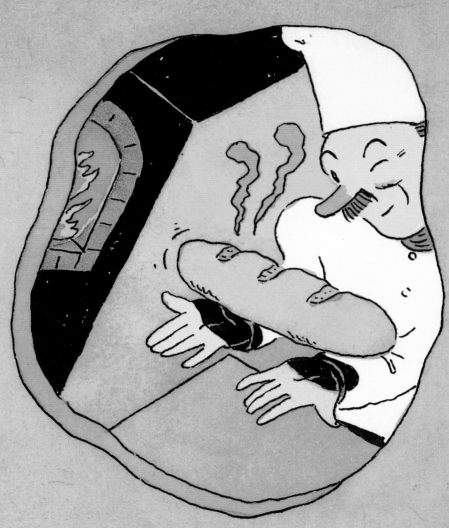

"Much better," said the farmer,
and he plucked a feather.
And off Peter ran to the baker.

"Look at this!" said the baker as he took a hot loaf
from the oven. "It's as light as a feather!"

Peter tucked the bread under his arm and hurried off
around the corner and up the street. There was his home.
And there was his father, waiting.
"Here I am," said Peter.
"Well," said his father, "those shoes may feel good,
but they're awfully slow."

"Yes," said Peter, wiggling his toes, "but they sure are smart."